Also by Inger Christensen

alphabet

Butterfly Valley

A REQUIEM

Inger Christensen

TRANSLATED BY SUSANNA NIED

A New Directions Book

The translator would like to thank Peter Borum, Denise Newman, and Thom
Satterlee for their help with these translations, and Declan Spring for his insightful
editing.

Grateful acknowledgment is made to the editors of the following books and journals
in which some of these poems were first published: "Butterfly Valley: A Requiem"
was published in Ireland by The Dedalus Press; "Watersteps" appeared in *Grand
Street*; "Poem on Death" appeared in *Tin House.*

Book design by Sylvia Frezzolini Severance
Manufactured in the United States of America
New Directions Books are printed on acid-free paper.
First published as a New Directions Paperbook Original (NDP990) in 2004
Published simultaneously in Canada by Penguin Books Canada Limited

Library of Congress Cataloging-in-Publication Data

   Christensen, Inger, 1935–
   [Poems. English. Selections]
   Butterfly valley : a requiem / Inger Christensen ; translated by Susanna Nied.
     p. cm.
   "A New Directions book."
     ISBN 0-8112-1579-2 (alk. paper)
   1. Christensen, Inger, 1935—Translations into English.
   I. Nied, Susanna. II. Title.
   PT8176.13.H727A6 2004
   839.81'174--dc22   2003025678

New Directions Books are published for James Laughlin
by New Directions Publishing Corporation
80 Eighth Avenue, New York 10011

Table of Contents

Butterfly Valley:
A Requiem

Butterfly Valley:
A Requiem

I

Up they soar, the planet's butterflies,
pigments from the warm body of the earth,
cinnabar, ochre, phosphor yellow, gold
a swarm of basic elements aloft.

Is this flickering of wings only a shoal
of light particles, a quirk of perception?
Is it the dreamed summer hour of my childhood
shattered as by lightning lost in time?

No, this is the angel of light, who can paint
himself as dark mnemosyne Apollo,
as copper, hawk moth, tiger swallowtail.

I see them with my blurred understanding
as feathers in the coverlet of haze
in Brajčino Valley's noon-hot air.

II

In Brajčino Valley's noon-hot air
where recollection crumbles, and all things
in the melding of plant segments and light
transform themselves from scentlessness to scent,

there I move backward, go from leaf to leaf
set them on nettles from my childhood's land,
the most divine of all of nature's snares
to capture what once flew away as days.

Here in its cocoon the admiral
once a spring-green, glutted caterpillar,
transforms itself to what we call a mind

so that, like other summers' butterflies,
it can bring the dense crimson hue of life
up from acrid caverns underground.

III

Up from acrid caverns underground
where first dream-creepers of the cellar darkness
and all the cruelty we would rather hide
form the foundation under the mind's depths,

up soar the Morpheus, the death-head, all
that turn their night-moth aspect outermost,
showing me how soft it is to fall
into ash-grayness and resemble god.

The cabbage butterfly from Vejle meadows,
that white soul on whose wing-mirror is drawn
the evanescent nature of all things,

what is it doing in this gloomy air?
Is it the grief my life has overtaken,
concealed by the perfume of mountain brush?

IV

Concealed by the perfume of mountain brush,
all blossoming is rooted in decay,
in tangle, shadow, and decomposition,
a labyrinthine, wild insanity,

just as the butterfly in flight conceals
the insect body to which it is bound—
we see it as a flower flying up
not as the rank iconoclasm it is—

as when an owl moth, sphinx moth, underwing,
whirling the characters of color past,
casts us a riddle to conceal the fact

that all the soul possesses for its hope,
beyond all, is the symmetry of sorrow, seen
as admirals, as blues, as mourning cloaks.

V

As admirals, as blues, as mourning cloaks
in the colors' periodic table scheme
assisted by the smallest nectar drop
can raise the earth up like a diadem,

as they, in color's clear lightheartedness,
in lavender, in crimson, lignite brown,
neatly encompass sorrow's hiding places,
although their life of joy is too soon done,

with butterfly proboscis they are able
to breathe the world as an image-fable
light as the gliding flight of a caress,

till every spark of love is used, and just
beauty's and terror's vying sparks remain,
as peacock butterflies are fluttering.

VI

As peacock butterflies are fluttering
I think myself in Eden's garden now,
but soon the garden sinks to nothingness
and even words, which once could be spelled out,

begin dissolving into the false eyespots
of checker, scarce copper, Harlequin,
whose magic words of silica-white nights
transform the light of day into moonlight.

Here gooseberry and blackthorn bushes grow;
whichever of the words you eat, they make
your life butterfly-easy to recall.

Perhaps I will cocoon myself and stare
at the white Harlequin, its sleights of hand
delusion for the universe's fool.

VII

Delusion for the universe's fool
is the belief that other worlds exist
that there are gods who bellow and roar
and call us random tosses of the dice;

but remind me of a summer day in Skagen
when in their mating flight the arctic blues
fluttered about all day like bits of sky
with echoes of the blue from Jammer Bay,

while we, who lay lost in hills of sand,
as numerous as only two can be,
allowed our bodies' elements to blend

with earth as fusion of the sky and sea,
two people who bequeathed to one another
a life that does not die like anything.

VIII

A life that does not die like anything?
How so, if in all our creation,
in nature's last, self-absorbed leaps, we see
ourselves in what is lost from the beginning,

we see the smallest particle of love,
of happiness, in a pointless process
enter the image of humanity
as grass, the very grass upon a grave.

What do we want with the great atlas moth
whose wingspan spreads a map of all the earth
resembling the brain-web of memories

that we kiss as our icons of the dead?
We taste death's kiss that carried them away.
And who has conjured this encounter forth?

IX

And who has conjured this encounter forth?
Is it my own brain, which is pale and gray?
Can it infuse light's colors with a glow
beyond that of the butterfly I saw?

I saw Aurora, its paprika splashes,
its pale sheen of savannah, pepper gray,
the painted lady's African migration,
direct route to the winterlands of earth.

I saw the buff-tipped moth's fine outline sketch,
black edges of its tiny half-moon shapes,
there at the wingpoint of the universe.

And what I saw was not just the far-fetched
imaginings a brain itself concocts
with peace of mind and fragments of sweet lies.

X

With peace of mind and fragments of sweet lies,
with downy sheen of emerald and jade,
the iris butterfly's bare caterpillars
can camouflage themselves as willow leaves.

I saw them eating their own images
which then were folded into chrysalis
hanging at last like what they simulated,
a leaf among the other clustered leaves.

When with their image-language, butterflies
can use dishonesty and so survive,
then why should I be any less wise,

if it will soothe my terror of the void
to characterize butterflies as souls
and summer visions of the vanished dead.

XI

And summer visions of the vanished dead—
the hawthorn butterfly that hovers like
a white cloud, splashed with deep pink traces
of flowers interwoven by the light;

my grandmother, enfolded in the garden's
thousand fathoms, stock, wallflower, baby's-breath;
my father, who taught me first names of all
the creatures that must creep before they die—

walk with me into the butterfly valley
where everything exists only apart,
where even the dead hear the nightingale.

Its songs glide with an oddly mournful lilt
from lack of suffering to suffering;
my ear gives answer with its deafened ringing.

XII

My ear gives answer with its deafened ringing,
my eye with its inward-turning gaze,
my heart is sure that I am more than no one,
but answers with the well-known little pain.

I see myself in winter moth, in umber
one evening in November's stand of oaks,
as they reflect the radiance of moonlight
and play the role of sunshine in dark night.

I am reflected in their pupal slumber,
their ruthless liberation when the need
is greatest in the mirrored rooms of cold,

and what I see for myself, the bereft,
bare mirror-gaze, is not just death—
this is a death that looks through its own eyes.

XIII

This is a death that looks through its own eyes
will see itself in me, for I'm naive,
a native who is bonded to the stark
self-insight in what we call life.

And so I play the role of black-veined white
fuse words with phenomena; I play
the fritillary caterpillar, gather
all the world's life forms into one.

Then I can answer death when it arrives:
I'm playing the brown wood nymph; dare I hope
that I'm an image of eternal summer?

I hear you well; you say that I am no one,
but I'm the one wrapped in an emperor's cloak
regarding you from wings of butterflies.

XIV

Regarding you from wings of butterflies
is just a little butterfly-wing dust
as fine as any nothing made by no one,
in answer to the leaves of distant stars.

Like light it swirls up in the summer breeze
like spark of pearl, like spark of fire and frost,
and all that exists in its vanishing
remains itself and never will be lost;

as copper, purple emperor, arctic blue
it turns the rainbow to earth's butterfly
within the earth's own visionary sphere,

a poem lesser tortoise-shells can bear.
I see a bit of dust begin to rise—
up they soar, the planet's butterflies.

XV

Up they soar, the planet's butterflies
in Brajčino Valley's noon-hot air,
up from acrid caverns underground
concealed by the perfume of mountain brush

as admirals, as blues, as mourning cloaks
as peacock butterflies are fluttering
delusion for the universe's fool:
a life that does not die like anything.

And who has conjured this encounter forth
with peace of mind and fragments of sweet lies
and summer visions of the vanished dead?

My ear gives answer with its deafened ringing:
This is a death that looks through its own eyes
regarding you from wings of butterflies.

Watersteps

Watersteps

I

1 The fountain in Piazza Nicosia was built in 1572. Jacopo della Porta was the architect in vogue at the time.

Piazza Nicosia isn't actually a plaza. It's part of Via di Monte Brianzo, widening in a northwesterly direction.

I sit at a table with place settings and glasses. They don't start serving until 1:00.

A red Jaguar drives into the square. It vanishes down Via Leccosa.

The sun shines. The water reflects the light. The paint of the red Jaguar reflected the light as it drove past.

2 The fountain in Piazza Colonna was sculpted from marble by Rosso dei Rosso in 1575. He came from Florence.

Piazza Colonna is dominated by a column (42 meters) with a twining relief that tells of Marcus Aurelius's victory procession.

I sit at a table with a hot cappuccino a glass and a pitcher of water.

A red Jaguar has stopped in the crosswalk. The light changes from *Alt* to *Avanti*. People look irritated.

The sun shines. The paint of the red Jaguar reflects the light. Cars block the view of the water.

3   The fountain in Piazza Campitelli could have been built by Jacopo della Porta in 1589. But it's not certain.

Piazza Campitelli stretches along Santa Maria on Campitelli. Alongside a nice restaurant.

I stand on the opposite corner between two ordinary buildings that belong to the municipality of Rome.

A red Jaguar zooms across the square. It comes from Via Campitelli and vanishes around the corner down Via Delfino.

The sun shines. The water reflects the light. The paint of the red Jaguar reflected the light as it drove past.

4   The fountain on Via del Progresso was built during Jacopo della Porta's second period in 1591.

Via del Progresso connects Via Santa Maria del Pianto with Lungotevere dei Cenci.

I sit on the steps of Santa Maria del Pianto. It's the only place you can sit.

A red Jaguar is parked at an angle outside the Palazzo Cenci.

The sun shines. The water reflects the light. The paint of the red Jaguar reflects the light.

5 The fountain in Piazza Farnese could have been built by Girolamo Rainaldi in 1628. But it's not certain.

Piazza Farnese is where it is because the Palazzo Farnese was where it was. There are actually two fountains. They're identical.

I walk around in the square.

A red Jaguar drives searchingly past the buildings.

The sun shines. The water and the paint of the red Jaguar reflect the light.

II

1   There are three steps up to the fountain in Piazza
    Nicosia. The fountain is octagonal and the upper basins
    rest on four dolphins.

    Piazza Nicosia is not famous. There's a post office there.

    I study a menu. *Pomodori ripieni*, stuffed tomatoes,
    something to start with, maybe seasoned with basil and
    mint.

    While the red Jaguar starts up and quickly drives away
    from Via del Progresso.

    While the sun shines and the water falls from the upper
    basins and splashes into the pool.

2   There is a railing around the fountain in Piazza
    Colonna. The pool is elliptical, broken by four concave
    curves. The dolphins are arranged on seashells. Two
    and two.

    Piazza Colonna is famous. On the facade of the Il
    Tempo building hangs the newspaper case. You can
    read there about the postal strike (*sciopero*).

My coffee is cold. The water glass drips. The sugar packet is wet.

While the red Jaguar drives into Piazza Campitelli for the third time in a row.

While the sun shines and the water falls and hangs like a veil from the basin in the middle of the pool. It's water that splashes. You can't see it for the cars. Nor can you hear it for the cars.

3 There is a lower railing around the fountain in Piazza Campitelli. It's made of three kinds of marble: the bottom pool grayish, the top basin pink, between them the white balusters.

Piazza Campitelli is neither famous nor unknown. It's well preserved.

In the corner between the buildings you look down into a narrow space with ruins and cats.

While the red Jaguar probably vanishes from Piazza Nicosia.

While the sun shines and the water falls from the pink basin into the gray pool and from the gray pool through the masks out into a drain channel in the edged platform. There are no dolphins. It's water that splashes.

4 There are two steps up to the fountain on Via del
  Progresso. It is made of marble which they say was
  taken from Nero's grave. There are masks but no dol-
  phins.

  Via del Progresso is not famous at this time. At this time
  it's fairly unimpressive.

  I light a cigarette.

  While the red Jaguar drives on because the light has
  turned green on Piazza Colonna.

  While the sun shines and the water falls from the upper
  basin and splashes into the pool.

5 There is a wrought-iron fence with gates that don't
  close around the fountain in Piazza Farnese. It is made
  of Egyptian granite originally used in Caracalla's
  baths. There are no dolphins but there are masks and
  lions. The lions sit on an extra pool. It is shaped like a
  bathtub.

  Piazza Farnese is famous because the Palazzo Farnese is
  famous.

  I look at the famous facade of the Palazzo Farnese.

While the red Jaguar drives away from Piazza Nicosia down Via Leccosa or away from Piazza Campitelli down Via Delfino or away from somewhere else in the city.

While the sun shines and the water falls from the upper basin through masks bathtub and lions to the big pool which is bowed as well as edged. It's water that splashes.

III

1 The four dolphins do not move in the fountain in Piazza Nicosia.

Because of the strike the post office is closed.

While I wait for strawberries with sugar and white wine.

While someone or other gets out of a red Jaguar in Piazza del Popolo.

Reporting that the sun shines the water falls and the paint on the red Jaguar reflects the light.

2 The four dolphins do not move in the fountain in Piazza Colonna.

Because of the strike you can read about the strike on the facade of the Il Tempo building.

While I wait to drink a little water from the dripping glass without having it drip.

While someone or other gets out of a red Jaguar in Piazza del Popolo/Piazza di Spagna.

Reporting that the sun shines the water and the paint fall and reflect the light.

3   The four masks do not move on the fountain in Piazza Campitelli.

Because of the strike you can find a letter among the cats down in the narrow space.

While I wait for some municipal employee or other to come out of the buildings that belong to the municipality of Rome.

While someone or other gets out of a red Jaguar in Piazza del Popolo/Piazza di Spagna/Piazza Barberini.

Reporting that the sun shines the water and the paint and the light fall and are reflected.

4　The four masks do not move on the fountain on Via del Progresso.

Because of the strike at this time no one is hearing of Via del Progresso at this time.

While I wait for the next cigarette.

While someone or other gets out of a red Jaguar in Piazza del Popolo/Piazza di Spagna/Piazza Barberini/Piazza Venezia.

Reporting that the sun and the water and the paint and the light shine and fall and are reflected.

5　The two times four masks and the two times two lions do not move on the two fountains in Piazza Farnese.

Because of the strike the Palazzo Farnese can be read like a letter.

While I wait for a letter from someone or other.

While someone or other gets out of a red Jaguar in Piazza del Popolo/Piazza di Spagna/Piazza Barberini/Piazza Venezia/Piazza della Repubblica.

Reporting that the sun and the water and the paint and the light shine and fall and splash and are reflected.

IV

1 The four dolphins begin to move.

   While the letters smell of white wine and sugar.

   While I think of Jacopo della Porta's many fountains.

   Reporting del Popolo Over Nicosia The red Jaguar.

   Reporting that the water is overflowing.

2 The four dolphins begin to move.

   While the letters drip water and the writing flows out.

   While I think of Rosso dei Rosso's memories of
   Florence.

   Reporting di Spagna Over Colonna The red Jaguar.

   Reporting that the sun is overflowing.

3 The four masks begin to move.

   While the letters belong to the municipality of Rome
   where the writing flows out.

While I think of the many fountains that Jacopo della Porta did not get to build.

Reporting Barberini Over Campitelli The red Jaguar.

Reporting that the light is overflowing and melting.

4   The four masks begin to move.

While the letters tell of writing that flows out.

While I think of Jacopo della Porta's opinion of Rosso's fountains.

Reporting Venezia Over del Progresso The red Jaguar.

Reporting that the paint is overflowing and melting.

5   The masks and the lions all begin to move.

While the Palazzo Farnese is read like a letter that flows out.

While I think of Rainaldi's opinion of Jacopo della Porta and Rosso.

Reporting Repubblica Over Farnese The red Jaguar.

Reporting melting.

V

1 While the dolphins dance all over Nicosia.

While the letters are opened and drunk like white wine.

Reporting Jacopo della Porta in The red Jaguar.

Reporting del Popolo Melting Nicosia

Over.

2 While the dolphins leap with the flood all over Colonna.

While the letters' flowing writing is drunk up and acts like white wine.

Reporting Rosso dei Rosso in the red Jaguar Over Jacopo della Porta in the red Jaguar

Reporting di Spagna Melting Colonna.

Over.

3 While the masks murmuring flow in the waters all over Campitelli.

While the letters' flowing writing is drunk up and acts like white wine.

Reporting della Porta Over dei Rosso Reporting della Porta 17 years later in the same Jaguar.

Reporting Barberini Melting Campitelli.

Over.

4 While the masks sing in the swirling bodies of water down del Progresso.

While the writing moves into the blood.

Reporting della Porta Over dei Rosso Reporting della Porta Over della Porta 19 years later in the same Jaguar.

Reporting Venezia Melting del Progresso

Over

5 While the masks and lions dance and sing and leap in a waterfall all over Farnese.

While the blood does the same

Reporting della Porta dei Rosso Over della Porta della
Porta reporting Girolamo Rainaldi in the same Jaguar.

Reporting Repubblica Melting Farnese.

Over

VI

1   While the dolphins dance in place and all Nicosia
    vanishes

    Reporting that the letters tell of del Popolo's fountains

    Reporting della Porta

    Melting Nicosia del Popolo

    Over

2   While the dolphins leap from fountain to fountain and
    all Colonna vanishes.

    Reporting that the letters tell of di Spagna's fountains.

    Reporting dei Rosso Melting della Porta

Melting Colonna di Spagna

Over

3 While the masks murmur of the dolphins' freedom and
all Campitelli vanishes

Reporting that the letters tell of Barberini's fountains

Reporting dei Rosso Melting Jaguar della Porta

Melting Campitelli Barberini

Over

4 While the masks sing of the masks' freedom and all del
Progresso vanishes.

Reporting that the letters tell of Venezia's fountains.

Reporting della Porta Melting dei Rosso della Porta
Jaguar

Melting del Progresso Venezia

Over.

5   While the masks and lions merge with the dolphins and
    all Farnese vanishes.

Reporting that the letters tell of Repubblica's fountains

Reporting della Porta Jaguar Melting dei Rosso della
Porta Rainaldi

Melting Farnese Repubblica

Over

VII

1   Reporting that the dolphins sit at a table drinking
    water: della Porta Nicosia del Popolo

2   Reporting that the dolphins drive a red Jaguar:
    dei Rosso Colonna di Spagna

3   Reporting that the masks smell of sugar and white
    wine: Jaguar Campitelli Barberini

4   Reporting that the masks drive a red Jaguar:
    del Progresso Venezia

5   Reporting that the lions read the red Jaguar like a letter:
    Rainaldi Farnese Repubblica

VIII

1 Dolphins masks and lions of marble

2 Smells sugar and white wine of marble

3 Red Jaguars of marble

4 Letters of marble

5 Water of marble

Poem on Death

Poem on Death

nothing has happened
>for days I sit
>>before the sheet of paper but
>>>nothing happens

*

I am like a child fed
>on sorrow
>>I lift my arm
>>>but can write nothing

I am like a bird that
>has forgotten its kind
>>I open my beak
>>>but can sing nothing

*

it feels so odd
>immodest to think
>>about death when no one
>>>you know has died

it means that each time
>you look at yourself in the mirror
>>you look death in the eye
>>>without crying

like a clear and fully
        comprehensible answer
                but to questions
                        you dare not ask

*

I can write nothing
        the sheet of paper empty as yesterday
                it seems so introverted
                        whitish and still

the same whitish color
        as snow grown old
                when the crust cracks
                        but nothing trickles out

nothing no tear
        no snowdrop nothing
                what if we did not
                        have to die

what if we always
        could be here on the earth
                which earthly condition
                        would we call death then

and which death call life
        when the blind person's soul
                has turned out the whites
                        of its eyes and sees

*

last night I dreamed
    that I died and came running
        with my dog
            into the kingdom of death

there was no one to be seen
    just stones a few bushes
        a landscape that travelers
            have often told of

as I said, I was dead
    but so tired that I soon
        fell asleep on a boulder
            and dreamed I died again

I preferred not to die
    here in death's darkness
        but in my own home
            where I had not died

so on the way back
    I stopped at the boulder
        for days I sat and
            wrote like this

all the death
    that an ordinary person
        must go through
            in the course of life

when I awoke I saw
        that nothing had happened
                the sheet of paper empty
                        but I breathed easily

*

it is lonely to think
        of death in December
                with the clouds shrouding
                        your house

in the park the threatening
        light beneath the trees
                all kinds of dead people
                        wandering the town

one with a fish
        that he sorrows over
                like a helpless thing
                        with tears of fishermen

one with the suffering
        bird that he carries
                over his heart
                        his deceased heart

one with a word
        that has lost its object
                the surviving words
                        that the body shakes off

the body whose blood
        runs away from its brain
            the body whose heart
                is cold as a knife

trapped
        between the stars
            we cry out
                from the coffin

words die
        on our lips
            the body is an animal
                that must die

in wild sorrow
        I suddenly remember
            the garden of Eden
                the open wounds of graves

the zinc-plated watering can
        the metal vase the rake behind the stone
            and the autumn sigh of starlings
                in gusts through the air

the sigh in which the worlds
        of the dead and not-dead
            meet in the comfort
                of the great desolation

*

write of death
        describe in a poem
                what you feel
                        about death

in the face of death
        I am like an animal
                and the animal can die
                        but can write nothing

try to write
        a poem about death
                has death a meaning
                        what

now that apples
        fall so far
                from the tree of knowledge
                        that they are not

eaten for pleasure
        nor from hunger
                but from weary greed
                        death is alone

now that apples look like
        models of apples
                ideal-apples
                        spotless

now that worms must gnaw
     at the breast of something
          other than children of man
              death is edged out

take death by the hand
     give it an apple
          walk up to its grave
              bite the apple first yourself

dance on its grave
     let wisdom rule
          devour layers of darkness
              followed by sunlight

words do die like flies
     their bodies everywhere swept
          from the white sheet of paper
              give dirt a little room

the newborn is like
     an ethereal creature
          not until stricken
              with illness does it seem

a human child
     give us room to love
          a mortal form
              of immortality

as depth lifts water
      up to a spring
           death lifts the living
                up to drink

Meeting

Meeting

I

I fear the impersonal between us, things we cast off without
tolerating or bearing, things whose stories we no longer
try to remember, and roads that go round and round
without anticipation

I fear the back, with a remnant of the pressure of metamor-
phosis still under its skin, with little nervous lights still
under closed eyelids, I fear the back

fear the clothes, the blankets, the closet door, everything
that conceals, even with life, with small movements and
openings in the flesh I fear the eyelid—won't open it
wide, don't want to see the back, and don't want to see
nothingness

I think we have sought wings on the back, I think we have
sought light in the eyes, sought places, along roads, each
other, God

this sloppy dishrag smack across the mouth, this vindictive
face, the grin and slamming doors—the pupil that lies in
wait in the dark and always claws the homecomer

this deep scratch in the throat, these shouts that repeat
overworked books rip them up with teeth without
hunger and swallow these tasteless pills prozil niamid
upharsin and mene mene nothing, while the moon-pot
pours and bright greasy gravy oozes over everything

what does it want, this opening in the lap—what does this cloth dog of childhood want, always sitting up, with arms, staring

I fear this cloth dog, the picture on the wall of mother and child, Picasso's dove of peace bigger than the earth, the calendar with shiny pages looking at us, our fear and flight, when we sweat each by himself

I fear this opening in the lap, try to close it—everything is like cactus and stone and backs and wires that cannot reach

what is meeting, now when we light a cigarette and look back, now when eyes no longer wait to look into eyes, only now and then secretly examine the other, the beloved other stranger—run the vacuum cleaner, turn pockets inside out, look your fill at a yellow pimple, one hair out of place and never reach the eyes

what is meeting—someone is dead, long live someone, the living room is a full card file, streetcars with their backs lined up, tattered cardboard boxes filled with detritus from the most recent thoughts' move, what is meeting till death do us part

will we come out then—is there an opening, wire, switch, when we suddenly find, and wings shall bear all that we do not, and death shall have no dominion

but dream—God—what is meeting, I take this comb to comb his hair, but he has a comb there in his hand, he puts this apple in my lap, but I am so full, oh autumn, drawers and boxes and the closed cover of the radio, I wanted to seek these roads, voices in the street like shining rails—who run into each other through the open jaws, is anyone left lying there, has everyone driven in, so the crane can swing them out over the edge

there should be a caution sign here, what does this death want before my eyes, why doesn't He turn his back, is he sick

I fear this sickness succeeding itself in us, this stinginess, the smell of sweat, take it away, it isn't like mine, the glob of phlegm in the washbasin, get it out—everything is catching, this Look what I'm giving you, so you'll never notice what I'm taking—give us a smile, come on, a great big one . . . ah, that was good, or the disappointment when it wasn't very big, but it was your own damn fault honey

honey lights another cigarette, looks back and down at a little dirt under her fingernails, fears the fine porcelain clock where the swallows no longer tick and the tense two-way switch that fills the whole living room conducts the current in separate directions, where we sit and cannot touch each other

fears the rusty bicycles that pedaled to the beach once, the dream again, yes but need, desire, and hope, wish, yes childishness, now when the ashes are shoved under the doormat and the shoe polish is long since used up

so far the door is locked and no one knows whether we have gone or come, whether this is a year or already the aftertime, what have you said to the others, to the men down on the corner, is there a corner, to whom have I

written about my heart as if it were a question of feel-
ings, did you read it all in the paper, to whom
I fear the back, the back that answers all questions without
mouth or eyes, with a coffee can's dogged innocence
and the ironing board's cold shoulders
has something been hidden, what has been hidden, what
lies hidden in the old suitcase with tags to and from, to
and from whom, what lies concealed at the bottom of
the dirty clothes hamper stifled under the pressure of
clammy and greasy and crawling, though we do not
have bugs, what is there in the bedclothes, what lies con-
cealed in my heart
don't stop, don't stop here, this obedient pumping, these
long hauls, hoist me up, pull me in over the edge, the
edge of the well, the box, whatever, the edge of the chair,
like that, yes, a little more, no for God's sake *a lot* and
hearing your voice: I think I'd like to sleep a little—or
was it mine, what is meeting
I fear the impersonal between us, this shrugging of the
shoulders, the back's grimaces, so long, so long, you
don't mind that, do you, and don't worry about it, it
doesn't mean anything—the priest with his back to the
congregation, is it always God he sees, oh turn, turn
around, say something
fear the old voices on the tape, no don't say anything, let us
see, see, see each other and You
what have I said, suddenly asked, entreated, implored,
begged—
oh this stubborn largish lump on the back, where the brain

runs down into the backbone, pressure of metamorpho-
sis, memory of salt on the lip after kissing, long stories,
creation, wind's confidences, the lap's wide opening
is someone coming toward me on the road
am I sitting with my face turned toward someone? R.S.V.P.

II

When morning stretches up again, when I again can touch
the telephone and dial out into the air, this is seagull-
wings—is that you yes screech and the daytime-win-
dows open distant all political unrest
there are still twelve gold-rusty asters left, one I found
bewitched sailing in the washbasin, water-wakening
miracle, who was wakened—and one lay face-down,
close to the newspaper stack, bled
twelve are left on the table full as if unfolded, what will
become of approaching unrest the buds the hours'
springboard and amount to something as if in one big
blossoming
I remember a black man's song that stripped all skin like
hate from our bodies, remember the gold-rust of his
voice's insanity-pump where water was soft as children
and the air-knife hard as sun
remember that the day has begun, this day, when yester-
day's dress is locked in the closet, the telephone book
hidden under the bed and the map of this metropolis
need not be used to get through again and again in vain
this day that holds the restless night in its hand like a shriv-
eled berry, a crumpled dial, will not use you any longer,
this zero zero five five just to hear a voice and what a
voice, Time, preacher without illusions 1:45:16 beep
again and again 2–3–4 something or other beep and
sleep

this day light the torch and pass it to one in chains melt his
fear which is mine with faith, throw the bread up high,
let it fly around the world and fall like manna on the
strangers, wing-bread here—is that you yes screech and
fill us up with your faith

oh germinal vision give them grain bread bread, oh
approaching unrest go away fill yourself with bread
bread, strip from us layer after layer of furs, crazy jew-
els and books, I mean paper, this bright paper industry,
this formless overgrown baby crying more and more
with its several hundreds of years—strip from us layer
after layer of the mind's conscious wanderings farther
and farther out but in ever smaller circles—strip this
poem of everything—grind it, mill it, flour, bread, faith

this poem—why don't I stop, you stand by my side conjur-
ing smiles, don't I understand even a smattering of the
whole—my poem which you will never see smatter
smatter—oh European times of beep beep beep, while
the black man sings, smiles smiles smiles

this poem this day if you stop the poem, you stop the day,
this poem draws nearer, seagull-wings, yes, speaking,
who's this—have you already risen from the ashes my
love of course I have the coffee ready

these words we say, be careful, still a bit of gold-rust which
must not lose its value, still the long stalks in water
when the stomach sinks, the opening, the faith must
never be closed

if you come like this and I come like this, with our backs to
all the hangovers of the past, overgrown hearts beat in

our bodies, fill our chests, stomachs, bulge from our
backs, as if far too much were included—grind it, heart!
new, steaming bread, daytime, still twelve asters and
aftertime of the miracle
meeting is always face-on

III

I do not know what it is. I cannot tell you what it is. I have
no clear concept; as with words, it is no longer clear
what they are.

Within the world. Once lost in the grass and always happily
crawling. One second the connection with evil lost and
always thoughts about some little approaching second or
other.

Care only about trees. They open out, fold in, close, stand
ajar. They have a tree-life, longer on the average. Trees
are also beautiful.

Care only about sea and sky and earth. The streaming, lift-
ing, bearing. The longest-living and all that moves with,
in, on; it is no longer clear what it is.

But it is within the world. We have stood up somewhere
and begin with steps. We press close to a tree to remem-
ber the grass. We press close to each other to remember
the tree. Step by step we go farther, try to remember the
body, press close to the wind and to space to try to see
what it is.

But it is no longer clear. We are within the world. Grass, tree,
body. Sea, sky, earth—care only about those. Nothing
has happened. But there is a silence. There is a lie. I can-
not say what it is.

Time sneaks kindly about. Streets blossom. Houses sway
like palms. Seagulls circle the holy flagpole. Everything
is in violent upheaval, like flowered dresses on tourist

boats. I have no clear concept. But bravely we say hello and goodbye or lay wreaths.

My love—for that word exists—there is a lie. There is a closed door. I can see it. It is gray. It has a little black hand to shake hello and goodbye. It has a little, black, stiff hand, which is completely still now. That door is not a lie. I sit and stare at it. And it is not a lie. I cannot tell you what it is.

IV

As we touched each other before, it was death we touched

as we pulled and pulled, each on his own side of the door,
it was death we held fast

held each other fast to the very end, closing time and no
deliveries, pain

until the door loosened its grip on us, opened up to us and
saw that we were gone

I fear this poem which is like a procession word after word
with their endings gone, what then?

this lie that we enter with leaf-fingers, grain-hair and flower-
breath, arms like lilies and bodies like swaying birches
and all that is fair in the world and suddenly faded

this lie that we enter again with the certainty of a lie: Laugh,
little children, like scythe after grain and eventually age
in young and old's favor and clap your small hands for
as long as you can

what then? I could address you, my love, write a letter from
a place, maybe even from a real place, if there is such a
thing, before dinnertime

oh world-place here, where it all could be born, bear with
my unrest, see the old wooden table with things that go
to or fro, it needs polishing, pull open the curtains, but
it is night

it is night, the window-rain glistens especially courteously,
outside hurries home on the bus for the redeemed, who
know where they are going

to a place, maybe, a real place

more and more to remember, this meeting you mentioned
today when we saw each other occurred precisely today
when we saw each other, just remind me of that

I hear them talk in the street; perhaps it is happiness talking,
without this dull procession of words, stammering in
sovereignty like rain and wind

here I must ask you to be careful, I am sorry to say it, but
world peace here, no, not here at all with this unrest in
the heart

and still we must sing, constantly with burning tongues,
come nearer earth, come nearer earth of man with your
hungering eyes, let not even death do us part, throw the
door wide for my love, sing in his body all people like a
real place

this lie of a procession, get rid of it, this lie of a life which has
come to rest in its life, get rid of it

steadily death makes its entrance through all our doors, all
streets and veins, let it in, do not let it run loose, do not
push it aside, but let it intervene, imply it

do not take it on your knee and look at it, but take day and
night, time, even place, take them on your knee and look
at us, as we open and close open and close oh—damn
the procession of words

this meeting you mentioned today occurred precisely today

V

The unknown is the unknown and gold is gold I've heard,
one winter the birds froze fast to the ice without the
strength to scream, that's how little we can do for words
with words

the books press close to one another and hold themselves
up, backs to the living room, our buttoned-up words
huddle on the shelf, the queue-culture of centuries, inex-
orably built up word by word, for who doesn't know
that the word creates order

order in the lump, the formless slime, the throng of pressing
eggs, here where we stand, order in the lumps in the
throats of all who speak, word after word that shoves its
way forward and always joins in at the right place or
stumbles over itself, another

like that, yes, it can be said like that and the word can stop
itself like a letter horrified by the distance alone

but it should not be said like that, we can still see it, we can
still see the great anonymous paper with all that
Rimbaud did not want to write

this great unfillable white square which never has been in a
picture by Jorn or of earth, but suddenly is there and
attracts the power of all your vision

and if you go outside all the earth sings like gold in your
ears and all their pictures rustle in your hand like our
wretched payments

if you go outside again all this is unknown unknown and

you can do so very little for the word your sister in this whitest land, a few birds left it in time

in time? —I think of a place where you lay with your head against a root like the felled trunk

I think of a seed in your hand that you carry in memory of a bird

I think of a green little fir still with growing tip foremost this tingling down through the trunk,

you sit like that evening after evening, while the light burns the words down to a flicker, darkness—are you unknown?

we walked on a stairway of snow with ice-floe hands and forest-edges chiming, close to each other

we flew through the house like peaks torn loose from mountain massifs no one has known

see the table down there with cups and clock and the dust that settled after our meeting

drawers, cubicles and beds, rooms full of clothes that we grew out of or just left behind in order to die with each other

but this acquiescence is suspect, no one takes root and when we suddenly waken in the night with a tightness: no one will die

above us looms the whiteness, the not yet fulfilled country of man, stretching its arms toward a sea we heard sighing when the tiredness came

above us looms whiteness—see what we have lost, like a winter

VI

I play it through to arrive at a point where the music meets
    resistance—to get rid of the resistance and meet the music
this house is again a colossus of slag, concrete with decom-
    posed bits of reeds from the low factory site, mortar
    with imprints of three great hands
these blinded eyes, this vaulted conglomerate of millions of
    eyes of workers from times and places—and the whip of
    gold like lightning over the roof
gold, my friends, like what hung from his belt, the glowing
    words that burned themselves into the middle of his
    body, when the sun and he rode the desert
I have imagined Rimbaud like that, with three great hands,
    two he used himself, the third used by the unknown
I have imagined music like that—oh these my two hands,
    which resist finding the third
again this house where a black man opens his eyes wide as
    beacons etching the air, where black men's blood has
    fertilized the aged abbey brick, where a fertility woman
    from a corner of the world in a corner of a temple in
    Mexico bore her screams here
down in the street the snow is a dirty border around a very
    common Scandinavian house with books, bath, and cen-
    tral heating, with only a slight contempt left over for
    what we have lost and heaped up
up here in the living room I search and search for my third
    hand; perhaps, hidden by snow, it has dug its way sin-

glehandedly, fumbled its way to the heart of this, is
    meeting my resistance at the innermost center of a poem
I play this through to arrive at a point, to arrive at nothing
    more afterward, to stand still for a moment point in a
    house in a world-body, ask for a moment impossible
    answers for my questions' impossible use—then again
    play through this impossibility point by point and pause
    by pause, toward the center of time when a parting let-
    ter could easily be sent before 10:00 a.m. when the mail-
    box is emptied
but a pretty little letter that does not rummage unnecessari-
    ly in what has happened was already sent four years ago
I forgot to tell you about a man in a white uniform who
    walked along the street in the snow in snow-white
    patent leather shoes and ditto mustache, bouquet in
    slightly outstretched left hand, as if nothing had hap-
    pened; I thought he was dead
I forgot to tell you that I think of your life as of death, that I
    again and again bury your body in my body, that I again
    and again set a deadline on your luck, which will not be
    tempted, tempt my poem, which . . .
if I could begin with a scream in a temple, again in this house,
    so that they all stood risen, all were lives in your life
life, my friends, that hung from his belt and flared up,
    burned down under Africa's sun
come again, my friends, and explain it again and again—it
    is pure gold and the shining unknown like the faith of
    someone who spoke of everything else
I think of your life, let this be innermost, let this be the cen-
    ter of my poem

VII

With my back to my poem, to myself, to my word, I go away
    from myself, from my poem, from my word, and even
    farther into my word, into my poem, into myself
through things we arrive at things, evening and morning in
    March, which is the march of days, departure upon
    departure, day after day, and it sounds like a procession,
    is one word only, march
evening and morning, already no more points in time but
    the mass of light careening in and out of itself, always
    the scream, when spinal cord is divided into spinal cord
    by spinal cord and all these people straighten up side by
    side, horsetail ferns swaying in the morning mist,
    Carboniferous Period by evening as we await the glow-
    ing fire, where the heart will begin to beat
who can think any longer of beauty, all the strangers move
    side by side in the one you love, if you offer your body to
    him it is the word you offer, which they do not under-
    stand—and who dares speak anymore of the beauty of
    understanding—if you offer bread, it is the people deep
    under the earth, high over the earth in mighty swaying
    flocks, who say thank you, go off and sit in the chair, read
    the paper and do not understand
but who dares speak anymore of the necessity of under-
    standing
I walked along a street once which turned into another
    street which turned into street after street I walked, I
    took hold of a hand

oh country of man, oh planet whirling swallowing spitting
swinging door is someone waiting in the wings, some-
one who is bigger, bigger than evil

this door constantly winging its way between evil and
good, this door that we rattle and think we have opened,
which always is opened and closed by itself alone

this mill that grinds and grinds, this poem that it opens and
closes like morning and evening at the same time and
what I myself wanted to place like a pretty ending from
one understanding to the other, I have forgotten

times, places forgotten, no longer mine, my love's,
strangers', no longer, no longer words', the proces-
sion's, no longer beauty's and evil's times and places,
but quite simply times and places streaming back and
forth through times and places, and people winging
around among people over and under endlessly back
and forth

one moment forgotten all evil in the world

do not believe in the lie, do not believe in oblivion, do not
believe in what is either here or there; believe in a per-
son, perhaps a random stranger, walking forth from his
strangeness, saying, I do not lie, it does not lie in me

believe that it is possible

that we have lost everything in meeting, my love—neither
death nor life

with our backs to death and life we go away from death and
life and farther and farther into death and life, play this
terrifying theme through, I think we have mentioned it
too often, in this our foreign language we have called it

love, I should mention it again and again, but words do
    not offer the same resistance as things
not the same resistance as hearts, lock them up, let them
    bleed through layer after layer of consciousness, these
    formless bastions of the ego, where fright wanders like
    an impersonal sheep with airy latter-day wool of spun
    glass as its only hopeless defense against what?
against a not yet fulfilled country of man, which we have no
    room to carry, against a house not yet built, which we
    have no time to live in, against the children not yet con-
    ceived in whom we dare not believe, write your name in
    their hearts and their names in your right hand
who dares speak anymore of the necessity of understand-
    ing, enough seen, enough owned, enough known and
    regardless of that the sun that burns and burns in the
    center of your body, through the child you dream, burns
    it down to a heap of sand easily whispered away like a
    word from your lips
oh my pain in your life
with my back to my back I will strip my faith down to my
    faith, with my back to the word, let words be words, let
    lies be lies, evil be evil—do not forget, but see him drag
    it behind him, the cross
believe that it is possible
who dares to speak anymore of the beauty of understand-
    ing, who dares to speak anymore of the center of a
    poem, as if it were a question of a poem, who dares to
    speak anymore of the beginning, face-on, as if it were a
    question of meeting

with our backs to our meeting we go away from our meet-
ing and farther and farther into our meeting, which is
things' meeting with things, which is times' and places'
meeting with time and place, which is morning and
evening in March, season and aftertime, opened and
closed, at the same time you and strangers

let me here at the brink of the whiteness, the unknown,
write a short message: to you, my love, neither life nor
death, but this word we use so often, in our foreign lan-
guage we have called it love.